This book belongs to
my friend:

_____

A NOTE TO PARENTS

Children are physically adventurous by nature, so minor scrapes and bruises are inevitable. In *Doctor Dora*, along with trusty Map and Backpack, Dora helps her friends feel better by patching up "boo-boos" and commending bravery.

This Dora adventure is filled with opportunities for your child to use his problem-solving skills. Ask your child what he would do to help each of Dora's friends feel a little better. Take this opportunity to talk about simple first aid for bruises, scrapes, and other minor medical emergencies. When Dora turns to Backpack for assistance, encourage your child to select the appropriate "fix it" item from Backpack before Dora does.

Children can often experience a bit of anxiety when it comes to small injuries or doctor visits. It is best to model reassuring and calm behavior in these instances. For instance, plan a special lunch for you and your child after a routine checkup. Keep a first aid kit easily accessible in your home and car. In addition to bandages, antiseptic spray, and cotton balls, fill your first aid kits with some inexpensive treats to have on hand to make those unexpected situations less painful.

Learning Fundamental: 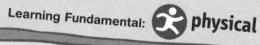 **physical**

For more parent and kid-friendly activities, go to www.nickjr.com.

Doctor Dora

ENGLISH/SPANISH GLOSSARY and PRONUNCIATION GUIDE

English	Spanish	Pronunciation
Eyes	Los ojos	LOHS OH-hohs
Ears	Las orejas	LAHS oh-REH-hahs
Heart	El corazón	EL koh-rah-SOHN
My	Mi	MEE
Arm	El brazo	EL BRAH-soh
Hello	Hola.	OH-lah
Thank you	Gracias	GRAH-see-ahs
Hand	La mano	LAH MAH-noh
You're welcome	De nada	deh NAH-dah
Nose	La nariz	LAH nah-REES
Yes	Si	SEE
Let's go!	¡Vámonos!	BAH-moh-nohs

Published by Scholastic Inc., 90 Old Sherman Turnpike, Danbury, CT 06816

SCHOLASTIC and associated logos are trademarks and/or registered trademarks of Scholastic Inc.

ISBN 0-7172-6638-9

Printed in the U.S.A.

First Scholastic Printing, July 2003

Doctor Dora

by
Samantha Berger

illustrated by
Susan Hall

SCHOLASTIC INC.

New York Toronto London Auckland Sydney
Mexico City New Delhi Hong Kong Buenos Aires

"I'm Doctor Dora. Are you ready for your checkup?"
Dora asked Boots one day.

Boots was the perfect patient. He let Doctor Dora
listen to his heart, check his eyes, and look in his ears.

"You're very healthy, Boots," Doctor Dora told him.
Just then, they heard a great big sound. AH-CHOO!
"That sounds like Benny sneezing!" said Boots.
"This is a job for Doctor Dora!" Dora exclaimed.

Eyes
Los ojos

Ears
Las orejas

Heart
El corazón

"First we have to find out where Benny is," Dora said.

"Map! Map!" Dora and Boots called.

Map popped out of Backpack's side pocket and said, "I can help you find Benny! First, go over Rock Bridge. Next, cross Rolling Rapids. Then, go through Red Rose Garden. That's where you'll find Benny!"

They started on their journey to find Benny.
AH-CHOO! they heard again.
"Poor Benny," said Doctor Dora. "We'd better hurry!"

"There's Rock Bridge!" called Boots.
They ran ahead and started climbing up the bridge.

But when they reached the top, there was Tico sitting on the ground holding his arm. He did not look very happy.

"Tico!" said Dora. "What happened to you?"

Tico shook his head and pointed at a loose rock on the ground. Then he held up his scraped arm. "*Mi brazo,*" he said softly.

"Tico must have tripped over that rock and scraped his arm," said Doctor Dora. "Don't worry, Tico. We can help make your arm feel better."

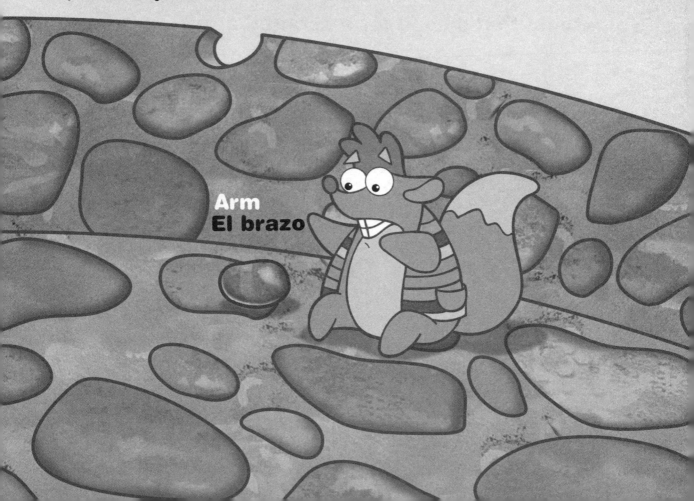

Arm
El brazo

"We need something to make Tico's arm feel better," said Doctor Dora. "I bet there's something in Backpack we can use."

"Backpack! Backpack!" called Dora and Boots together, and their friend Backpack sprang into action.

"*¡Hola,* Backpack!" said Doctor Dora. "We need something that's good for a scraped arm."

A bandage was the perfect thing! Dora put the bandage on Tico's arm to help keep it clean and gave Tico a lollipop for being so brave.

Tico smiled and said, "*Gracias*, Doctor Dora."

Then Boots picked up the rock that Tico had tripped over and set it back into Rock Bridge.

"No one will trip over that rock again," Boots said.

Dora and Boots waved good-bye to Tico and continued on their way.

AH-CHOO! AH-CHOO! AH-CHOO! The sneezes were louder than ever.

"We'd better go find Benny!" Doctor Dora said.

Rolling Rapids was next. But how would Dora and Boots get to the other side?

"I know! I know!" shouted Boots. "We can swing across!"

Dora and Boots grabbed onto vines, and together they swung across Rolling Rapids.

"We made it!" Dora exclaimed.
But Boots had one little problem.

"Ouch," he groaned. "My hand hurts."

Doctor Dora took a look at her patient's hand.

"Hmm . . . Boots, it looks like you have a thorn stuck in your hand. I think I can pull it out if you hold still."

"I'll try," Boots said, wanting to be brave.

Hand
La mano

"I'll count to three and then pull it out, okay Boots?" Doctor Dora asked.

"Okay," said Boots, closing his eyes.

"One, two, three," Dora counted and pulled out the thorn.

"I'm ready," trembled Boots, with his eyes still shut.

"I already took it out!" Doctor Dora laughed. "And here is a lollipop for being so brave."

"I didn't even feel it!" Boots giggled. "Thanks, Doctor Dora."

"*¡De nada!*" said Dora, and they were back on their way.

AH-CHOOOOO! By now the sneezing was so loud that the whole ground shook.

"Come on, Boots!" shouted Dora. "There's Red
Rose Garden!"
But where was Benny?

"Benny!" Dora and Boots called.

"AH-AH-AH-CHOO! Hi,"sniffled Benny. "I'm trying to pick roses for my grandmother's birthday, but it sure is hard with all the AH-AH-AH-CHOO . . . sneezing!"

Nose
La nariz

"I think Backpack has just the right thing for the sneezes," Doctor Dora said.

"Backpack! Backpack!" shouted Boots.

Dora gave the tissues to Benny. "Thank you, Doctor . . . AH-CHOO! . . . Dora," sneezed Benny, as he blew his nose like a trumpet.

Doctor Dora gave Benny a purple lollipop to make him feel better. Then she asked, "Benny, could the roses be making you sneeze?"

There was only one way to find out. Benny bent down and took a deep breath. "AH-CHOOOOOO!" He sneezed the loudest sneeze of all.

"Benny, we need to get you out of this garden!" Dora exclaimed. Just then Tico drove through the garden. "Tico, can you give us a ride?" Dora asked.

"*Si*," said Tico. "*¡Vámonos!*"

"*Gracias*," Dora said. "Let's go!"

They drove out of Red Rose Garden as fast as they could. Benny stopped sneezing.

"Phew! I feel better already," Benny said.

Everyone cheered, so nobody noticed the rustling sound behind them.

Before anyone could stop him, Swiper dashed in,
swiped Benny's bouquet, and disappeared.

"Oh no!" Benny cried. "Now I don't have flowers for
my grandmother's birthday."

"Don't worry," Dora reassured him. "I bet Backpack
has something you can give to her."

"Thanks, Backpack," Benny laughed, as he skipped off with some balloons. "And thanks, Doctor Dora."

"*De nada,*" Dora called after him.

Dora and Boots began walking home when suddenly they heard a loud AH-CHOO!

"Who could that be?" Boots wondered.

Just then Swiper appeared. "AH-CHOO!" he sneezed. "Oh mannn!"

"I guess Benny isn't the only one who sneezes when he's near red roses," Dora said.

And she and Boots laughed and laughed all the way home.